I0788382

You're Not Here By Accident!

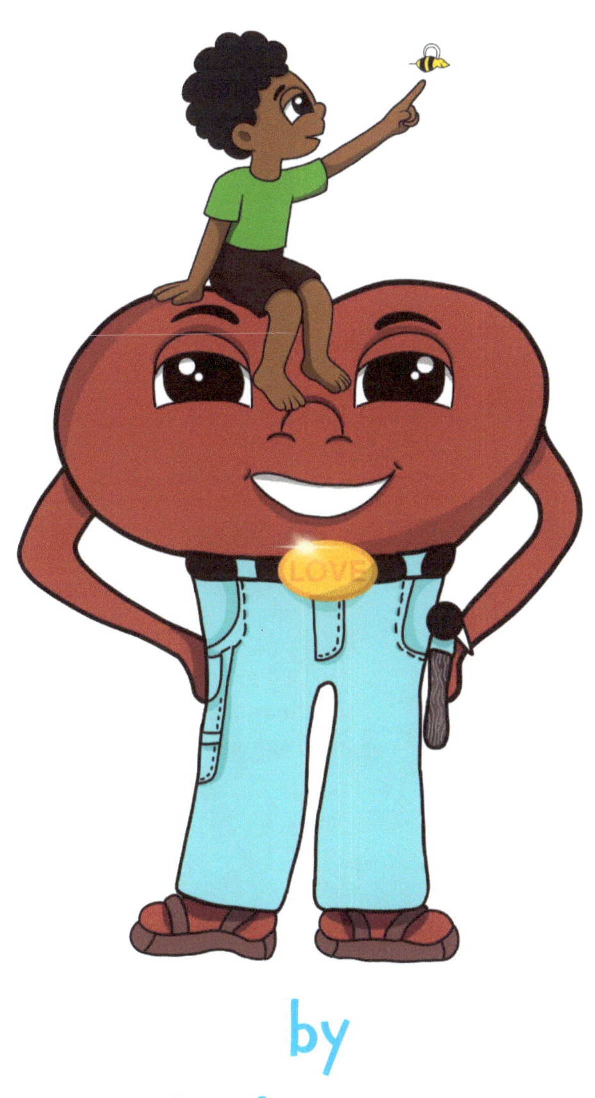

by

Nicole Deanes

ISBN: 978-0-9891348-4-2

Liberation's Publishing House - Columbus Mississippi

This book is dedicated to my children
and grandchildren.

In the heart of a child is a great place to be.
Hidden there you are invincible!

~Nicole Deanes~

"Children are a gift from the LORD;
they are a reward from him"
- NLT Psalm 127:3

You're not here by accident,
no, not by far.
Love had you on His mind

before there were stars!

Yes! It's true,
though hard to believe.
Love had you on his mind

before there were **Bees!**

Yes! It's true,
though hard to believe.
Love had you on his mind

before there were Bees!

Before there were **rivers**
with green
grassy banks...

Love had you on His mind

when earth's canvas was blank!

You are wonderfully and fearfully **designed...** by a wonderful loving divine **mind!**

That's right. I've **Declared** it!
Now believe that it's so!

Destiny awaits you.
Come on let's go!

What's that you say?
There's no mom or dad,
And being without them
does make you sad.
Let me tell you a secret

to put a smile on your face.

Even your parents couldn't

keep Love away.

Latter Rain Children's H

Love ordered you here on your

Birthday

not a moment, not a minute,
not a second too late!

Oh look at your face

so rosy and **Bright.**

Look at those limbs

there's a left and a right.

Accidents don't produce

such **Beautiful Things.**

Accidents don't

laugh, dance, clap, or **Sing!**

No! **You're** not here
by accident,
no, not by far.
Love had you on his mind
before there were **Stars.**

LOVE

Write Your Goals